Snow White

Key sound **aw** spellings: a, augh, aw, ough, or
Secondary sounds: igh, ake, nd

Written by Nick Page
Illustrated by Clare Fennell

Reading with phonics

How to use this book

The **Reading with phonics** series helps you to have fun with your child and to support their learning of phonics and reading. It is aimed at children who have learned the letter sounds and are building confidence in their reading.

Each title in the series focuses on a different key sound. The entertaining retelling of the story repeats this sound frequently, and the different spellings for the sound are highlighted in red type. The first activity at the back of the book provides practice in reading and using words that contain this sound. The key sound for **Snow White** is aw.

Start by reading the story to your child, asking them to join in with the refrain in bold. Next, encourage them to read the story with you. Give them a hand to decode tricky words.

Now look at the activity pages at the back of the book. These are intended for you and your child to enjoy together. Most are not activities to complete in pencil or pen, but by reading and talking or pointing.

The **Key sound** pages focus on one sound, and on the various different groups of letters that produce that sound. Encourage your child to read the different letter groups and complete the activity, so they become more aware of the variety of spellings there are for the same sound.

The **Letters together** pages look at three pairs or groups of letters and at the sounds they make as they work together. Help your child to read the words and trace the route on the word maps.

Rhyme is used a lot in these retellings. Whatever stage your child has reached in their learning of phonics, it is always good practice for them to listen carefully for sounds and spot words that rhyme. The pages on **Rhyming words** take six words from the story and ask children to read and spot other words that rhyme with them.

The **Key words** pages focus on a number of key words that occur regularly but can nonetheless be tricky. Many of these words are not sounded out following the rules of phonics and the easiest thing is for children to learn them by sight, so that they do not worry about decoding them. These pages encourage children to retell the story, practising key words as they do so.

The **Picture dictionary** page asks children to focus closely on nine words from the story. Encourage children to look carefully at each word, cover it with their hand, write it on a separate piece of paper, and finally, check it!

Do not complete all the activities at once – doing one each time you read will ensure that your child continues to enjoy the stories and the time you are spending together. **Have fun!**

Princess Snow White, skin like snow,
had a stepmum, long ago.
Every night, this queen would call
to her mirror on the wall:

"Mirror, mirror, on the wall,
who's the fairest of them all?"

The mirror says, "I speak true,
fairest of them all is you."

Snow White grows up
fair and kind.
One day, Queenie
speaks her mind,
"Mirror, mirror,
on the wall,
who is the fairest
of them all?"

The mirror says,
"I speak right.
Fairest of them all?
Snow White."

Queenie's heart goes cold as water.
She sends a man to kill her daughter.
He takes Snow White to the wood
but lets her go: his heart is good.

In the woods, she finds Small Hall,
a house for someone not very tall.
She calls "hello", then knocks at the door.
But no one's home. "Shall I explore?"

Hello!

Stay!

Stay!

Tired, she falls asleep in a chair.

Seven dwarfs come in. "Who's that there?"

She tells her story and they say, "Right!

stay in Small Hall, if you like."

Back at court, a week goes by.
Queenie gives her normal cry:
"Mirror, mirror, on the wall,
who's the fairest of them all?"

The mirror says, "You're all right,
alternatively, there's Snow White."

Queenie bawls and Queenie roars,
"Still alive! Well, this means war!"

She chants a spell and then – surprise!

She's small and old – a great disguise!

Grabs her cloak and shawl and more,

a rosy apple with poisonous core.

Finds Small Hall and there's Snow White!

"Try my apple – take a bite!"

She snorts with glee, as Snow White falls:

"Now I'm the fairest of them all!"

When the dwarfs came home, they found Snow White lying on the ground.

How they cried – they all adored her.
They built a coffin and, in it, stored her.

16

Back at court, the queen transforms,
and takes again her usual form.
**"Mirror, mirror, on the wall,
who's the fairest of them all?"**

The mirror sighs, "You're fairest of fair.
Snow White's gone – what more do I care?"

A prince rides by and sees Snow White.

"She must be mine!"

(It's love at first sight.)

They lift the coffin, then they stumble
and out of her mouth, the apple tumbles.
A yawn. A stretch. She lifts her head.
She's reborn! Snow White's not dead!

Meanwhile, Queenie has a thought –
she asks the mirror to report:
"Mirror, mirror, on the wall,
who's the fairest of them all?"

The mirror says, "Cue applause,
it's Snow White! She shoots! She scores!"

The queen goes mad, she turns all red,
her hair falls out, she drops down dead.

21

The prince asked Snow White for her hand
and all the dwarfs, a song they sang.
"Mirror, mirror, on the wall,
who's the fairest of them all?"

The mirror said, "I speak right,
fairest of all is, forever, Snow White."

Key sound

There are several different groups of letters that make the **aw** sound. Read the words and use them in questions for the magic mirrors. For example: Mirror, mirror, on the wall, will I ever go to a ball? What do you think the mirror would reply?

all
fall
wall
ball
call
small
hall
tall

form
transforms
snort
short
story

yawn

shawl

bawled

scrawled

straw

naughty

daughter

caught

taught

four

court

courtyard

pour

25

Letters together

Look at these groups of letters and say the sounds they make.

igh **ake** **nd**

Follow the words that contain igh to help Snow White find love at first sight.

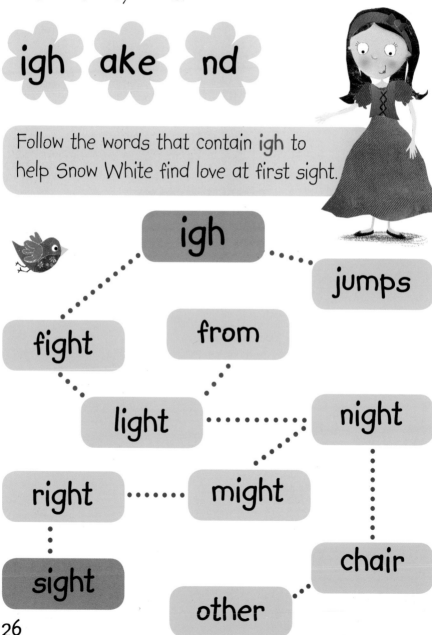

igh

jumps

fight

from

light

night

right

might

chair

sight

other

Follow the words that contain **ake** to help Snow White bake a cake.

ake

make

the

bake

lake

flake

rake

other

shake

cake

lots

Follow the words that contain **nd** to reach a happy ending.

suddenly

send

nd

band

land

pretend

ending

bend

mend

27

Rhyming words

Read the words in the flowers and point to other words that rhyme with them.

kind	**snow**	low
grow		wall

apple	**queen**	seen
shawl		been

ball	**wall**	tall
mirror		home

since	prince	water
report		mince

mirror	hand	queen
band		sand

coffin	yawn	lawn
shawl		dawn

Now choose a word and make up a rhyming chant!

I **yawn** at **dawn** on the **lawn**.

Key words

Many common words can be tricky to sound out. Practise them by reading these sentences about the story. Now make more sentences using other key words from around the border.

A **man** took Snow White to the woods.

Snow White lived **with** the dwarfs.

The queen **asked** her mirror who was the fairest of all.

Snow White and the prince **had** a party.

because • they

• trees • bad • tea • eyes • white • they • dark • looking

The apple fell out **of** Snow White's mouth.

The mirror **told** the queen Snow White was alive.

Along came a prince.

The queen **gave** Snow White a poisoned apple.

The dwarfs made a coffin **because** they adored Snow White.

When the dwarfs came home, **they** found Snow White on the ground.

along · this · now · we · all · of · good · know · man · told · never · gave · asked

with · back · had · she · too · some · people · into ·

Picture dictionary

Look carefully at the pictures and the words.
Now cover the words, one at a time.
Can you remember how to write them?

apple   coffin   core

daughter   dwarfs   hair

hand   man   mirror